Back Door Pass

THE DR. CAGE CHRONICLES:
MEMOIRS OF A SEX THERAPIST

Back Door Pass

GRAYSON ACE

4 Horsemen
Publications, Inc.

Chapter 1

After what happened during Bruce's appointment, I realized that having interns in my practice may not have really been the greatest idea. Even without having a job posted for new interns, I was literally receiving over fifty emails a day from college students wanting to come work for me, and I knew the guys had to have been telling them about how the internship "worked." I didn't want to get rid of them completely, so I told them we would be taking a bit of a break so they could focus on prepping for their finals, and that we would pick back up the following semester.

After a day like that, I was super thankful that it was the weekend. I just wanted to go do some shopping, get something to eat, and then go home a plop my ass down on the couch and binge some shows. I texted Jackie to see if she wanted to meet at the mall, but she was stuck at work, so I locked up the office and headed out anyway.

I hadn't been back to this mall since the day I met Nick acting as Santa Claus. It's funny how the mall is a lot less busy when there's not this sexy Santa's muscles busting through that red jacket. Although with him gone, apparently all eyes were on me, because I had this weird sense come over me that everywhere I went, people were staring and talking about me. This mall was full of gays, and my unorthodox practices were no secret in the community. It didn't bother me though–I was basically a walking billboard, and at this rate, just walking through the mall would increase my client base.

I was nearing 200 clients in my books, and with what I charge for a session, well, you can do the math. I wasn't hurting for money. I thought about hiring another therapist or even expanding my practice to a second location, but I felt like that would take away from the specialty services that I offer. People came to me for a reason. If I had more therapists, they wouldn't necessarily come back and pay what I charge.

A lot of people considered my process to be prostitution, but I didn't see it that way at all. I don't have a sexual interaction with *every* patient—just most of them. But they are truly coming to me for professional help, and I have yet to have a patient say that my services failed what they were looking to accomplish.

I continued walking through the mall, just doing some window shopping, and trying to ignore all the guys looking at me. At one point, this cute guy walked up to me and just said, "Can't wait to see you next week!" And then he ran off. I didn't recognize him, but I could only imagine what he was thinking about. I went to the food court and grabbed a smoothie, and just as I always did, nonchalantly dropped a few business cards right outside of the men's bathroom. It was no secret that the mall bathrooms were a popular cruising spot, and one business card certainly seemed to go quite a long way.

I got home, plopped down on the couch, and started surfing through the channels. It was getting late, and I wanted to relax but wasn't quite in the mood. Nothing on the tv seemed to be sparking my interest, so I threw the remote onto the table and picked up my phone to start scrolling through social media. I stumbled upon Nick's post—a typical naked man dancing on stage, and the caption just said, "Don't miss it." It was an advertisement for some party tonight at Swinging Richards. I wasn't really in the mood to go out but was also bored just lying on the couch, so I figured what the hell. I took a quick shower, threw on some clothes, and ran out the door. I had no idea what I was about to get myself into.

Chapter 2

I showed up to Swinging Richards, and the place was already packed with a line of probably a hundred people out the door. I knew a lot of the guys who worked there, so they just let me in without waiting in line. Plus, a few of them were my clients. I made my way through the crowd and back toward the end of the bar where I normally hung out and ordered my usual drink. There was already a duo dancing on the stage, one shaking their ass and the other pulling up some guy from the crowd's face into his cock. You know, the typical stuff that happens here on a Friday night.

I saw Nick walk out from one of the dressing rooms and head toward the stage, and of course he saw me. And damn, he looked fine as fuck. He already had his shirt off and was just wearing a super thin jock strap, and I could see that the head of his cock was practically bursting out of it. He smiled and waved as he walked to the stage, and I knew he was going to try and talk to me after his performance. Even though he could be pretty annoying, God was he hot!

Nick got up on stage and started dancing, and I have to admit, even from a distance, he was turning me on. I could feel my own cock start to tingle as he started grinding his on the pole. He normally did his dances with two or three other guys on stage, but this time he was solo, and he owned that stage. I closed my eyes for a second because from the way he was moving his hips, I wanted to imagine what he would be like in bed.

He finished his show and walked off the stage, and I knew he was going to be walking over toward me, and for once, I was actually going to entertain his conversation. I knew he was in love with me from our few minimal encounters, but there was no way I could ever have a relationship with a stripper. I saw him walking toward me, but then three guys came running over in front of him to talk to me.

"You're Dr. Cage! Oh my God!" one screamed. I wasn't even paying attention, and I was trying to see where Nick went to without being rude to these guys. I looked over one's shoulder and saw Nick walking the other way with his head down. The three guys kept rambling on, and I heard one of them mention something about an internship and another say something about an appointment, but I really wasn't paying attention to them. I kind of kept nodding my head and smiling but was really more focused on where Nick had gone.

The three guys eventually got sidetracked with the next performer who went on stage and ran off to watch, finally leaving me alone. I wanted to find where Nick had gone to, and then I saw him come out of one of the showers and drying himself off. I finished my drink and started walking over toward the back of the bar where he was.

"Hey, it's good to see you." I walked up and gave him a hug. He wrapped his muscular arms around me, and for a moment I couldn't hear anything—he had some really magical arms. His towel was about to fall off, but I grabbed it for him because he didn't seem to be paying attention.

"There's a, umm, special event going on tonight. You want to join. I think you'll enjoy it." I had no clue what he was talking about, but I just shook my head in agreement, and he grabbed my hand to follow behind him. He pulled me up ahead of him and pointed to the door at the very end of the hallway. "That's where we need to go."

I walked up to the door, and he reached around me to enter the code to unlock it. Just as the door opened up, his manager came running down the hallway and grabbed Nick's arm to pull him away. I turned around and watched as he walked away, and I head the manager say something about a VIP who had just arrived. Nick kept looking back, and I could tell he didn't want to leave me, but I knew he couldn't refuse the VIP.

I turned around to see what was going on behind the door that had just opened, and my jaw completely dropped.

Chapter 3

Fucking. Thrusting. Humping. Sucking. Moaning. Everything.

There had to have been at least a dozen guys in the room. Nick wanted to take me to an orgy. And I wasn't mad about it.

I stood in the doorway for a few minutes, just watching what was going on in front of me. I mean, I had been in some group situations before, and even just this morning, but nothing that I would have ever considered an orgy. This. Now—this was an orgy. I really just needed a minute to comprehend what was going on and decide where I would fit in.

In one corner, some beefy guy had two guys bent over in front of him, going back and forth between eating their asses out and fingering the other. On a couch in the center, one guy was riding another, while the top was sucking on some dick. There was a mattress on the floor in the middle of the room where four guys were doing a train on each other, and over in the other corner, two guys were down on their knees sucking on this massive hung cock.

I was so in awe that I didn't even realize there was a guy sitting at a table right next to the door I had walked through.

"Top or bottom?" I looked at him, almost like I didn't understand what he said.

He asked me again, "Top or bottom?" And again, I just looked back at what was going on in front of me. The guy got up out of his chair and said, "First time, huh?" And I just shook my head, still looking at the greatness I was about to jump into.

"I need to know if you're a top or a bottom."

"Uh, neither. Wait. Both. I'm verse."

And the guy gave me a green wristband and explained that all of the guys have a wristband which goes with their preference. Green is verse. Red is top. Yellow is bottom.

I put on the wristband and ripped off my clothes, deciding I was just going to start in one corner and attempt to make my way through the entire thing, that is, if I could hold out that long.

I walked over to the guy who was getting his dick sucked by the other two guys and just started making out with him. I grabbed onto the back of one of the sucker's heads so I could feel him moving back and forth, and he instantly moved my way and started sucking on my cock. We kept making out, and after a minute, he dropped down to his knees and pulled my cock out of the other guy's mouth and started slobbing on it. I leaned into the corner, and all three of them were taking turns on my dick. One would start sucking on my balls while the other two licked up and down my shaft.

For a second, I thought to myself, *why even go to another group? These guys know what they're doing.* I wasn't really sure how an orgy was supposed to work, if you were supposed to stay with your group and make your way around, but once one of the guys stopped sucking on my dick and ran to the other side of the room, I knew that movement was okay.

I started looking around to see where I wanted to go next, and the mattress was calling my name. I was in a bit of a bottoming mood, so I got down on the mattress in the front of the line and backed my way in. The guy in front pushed me forward a little bit, and I felt him shove his tongue down my hole. He was licking and fingering me, getting it nice and loose, then he grabbed onto my hips and pulled me back until I felt his head press against me. He was obviously a gentle guy because rather than shoving his cock in, he let it slide in naturally, and I'm glad he did because I could tell he had a wide one.

He held onto my hips while he started pounding away, and it was almost like I could feel the guy thrusting behind him. He would reach around and stroke my cock and kept leaning forward to suck on my neck and ears. I let him go at me for a few minutes, and then all of a sudden, the guy who was sucking my dick in the corner came over and knelt down in front of me, pulling my head down into his junk and shoving his cock in my mouth.

I was starting to realize that the wristbands were the only rules in an orgy, and anything else goes. It was actually a bit of a nice feeling, knowing that you didn't have to have some conversation and could kind of just do whatever you wanted. I could feel his cock destroying my throat, and I kept sucking on it as hard as I could.

He backed up and turned around, and I was surprised to see him start backing his ass into me—he was wearing a red wristband, which meant he was a top. As he backed into me, he grabbed my cock and aimed it for his hole, saying, "I normally don't do this, but you're hot as fuck." I rammed my shaft straight into his hole and grabbed onto his shoulders, shoving every ounce of energy I had into his hole. For a top, he sure was loose, and I'm assuming I wasn't the first guy who had been in him tonight.

I was still determined to make my way around the room, and it seemed like more people were just staying put. I get it—once you're in the motion, it can be hard to stop. I walked over to the couch where the one guy was still riding the other's cock, but the third guy had moved on to something else. I knelt down in front of the couch and started licking the bottom's hole as he was getting drilled. I would move from the hole to the cock and back again but wanted to make sure his hole was nice and wet.

I stood up and leaned in to whisper in his ear. "Want two?" He turned around and nodded his head with a smile on his face. I spit in my hand to get my cock nice and wet, and he stopped bouncing to give me a chance to get in. I pressed the head of my dick against his hole, and he leaned forward to give me a little more room. I could tell the other guy's cock was massive, so I knew this was going to really stretch him out. I got my shaft about halfway in when he started moving his ass back and forth, and then I felt him reach around and spread his cheeks a bit, allowing his hole to swallow the rest of me.

The top started thrusting again, and his cock rubbing against mine damn near made me blow, but I was really concentrating to hold it because I wanted to make it over to the final group. I grabbed onto the guy's shoulders and took control, pounding away while the other top stopped thrusting. I couldn't even believe that I was able to get in and out with the other anaconda taking all the space, and after about two minutes of hard fucking I heard the top yell, "I'm cumming!"

I could feel his monster start throbbing as it was shooting his load deep in his hole, and I could feel it all over my cock. I pulled out of his ass, and the little bottom jumped off the ride and got down and started sucking every last drip out of the dude's dick. At this point, I was close to bursting but was ready for the final round.

I walked over to the other corner, and the big beefy guy was still eating ass while the other guy was just sitting in a chair next to them jerking off. I got down on my knees and took his cock from his hand and started sucking on it. He was a bottom, but apparently the colors don't always mean everything. As I was slobbing on his tool, I felt a warm tongue start gently moving around my hole. I was stroking the guy's cock and turned around and saw the big beefy guy behind me.

"Fuck me, now." The beefster didn't waste any time, and he spit on my hole and shoved himself deep inside. I started sucking on the dick again, and the guy was going so hard on me he was pushing the chair that the guy was sitting in. Another guy had come over and laid down in front of me so I could start fucking his face. The guy fucking me suddenly stopped and held his body still, and then I could feel his dick unloading inside of my hole and filling me up. I kept sucking really hard on the other guy's cock until he started blowing in my mouth and I could swallow every last drop.

I could still feel the guy's hard dick in my ass, and the other guy was still sucking on my cock. I grabbed his head and pulled him up and told him to lay down on his back so I could fuck him.

"No dude. I don't bottom."

"I don't care. I'm about to blow my load, and I'm not wasting it on your mouth. Let me have your hole." I pushed him over so he was on his back. He just looked at me and smiled, then grabbed his legs to held them back.

I probably was only halfway in his hole when I felt my cock unleash that built up load into his ass, and I started pounding as hard as I could to empty it out, the guy behind me still as hard as a rock. I could still feel his cock sliding against my insides as I was thrusting away at this top, and I felt him grab onto my hips to pull my ass hard into his dick. He was cumming again, and this time, it was exploding out of my hole.

He kept his dick in me for another minute, and I could feel him forcing his jizz into me. When he finally pulled his monster out, I could feel his load falling out of my loose hole, and the top that I had just filled up scrambled around me and started eating my hole.

I eventually laid down on the floor, exhausted at the experience I had just had. I looked over, and it actually looked like a few more people had joined the room. I got up and walked over to the guy manning the door and handed him back the wristband, but he told me to keep it, just in case I wanted to come back. I grabbed my clothes and put them on, and as I opened the door, Nick was standing right there with a bit of a shocked look on his face.

"Thanks, Nick." I gave him a kiss on the cheek, and I ran off.

Chapter 4

I did absolutely nothing for the rest of the weekend. In fact, I didn't even wake up the next day until around 4pm, but all I could think about was that experience—my first orgy. Part of me wanted to go back to the club to get some more. I couldn't even remember the last time a guy came in my ass twice, or if it had ever even happened to me before. Part of me was a little bummed out that I didn't get any of their numbers. I'm sure I could have asked Nick for them, but would that be weird?

Shit. What about Nick? I mean, he was taking me into that room anyway and didn't say anything when his boss came to get him. I wondered if he was pissed that I stayed instead of leaving and waiting for him. But how could he have expected me to walk away after seeing what I saw? I was even a little bit confused as to why he even took me to that room. Did he just want to watch me fuck someone else? Was he into that? Or did he want to fuck me with others watching? A million thoughts must have run through my head, but I guess it really didn't matter.

The following night I was just about to jump into bed when I heard someone knocking on the door. I ignored it, but whoever it was just kept pounding on the door. I yelled for Rocky to answer it, but the person just kept pounding and Rocky was ignoring me. I jumped out of bed and grabbed a pair of shorts, so I wasn't running through the house naked. I swung open Rocky's door and was about to yell when I realized he wasn't home. I ran down the stairs and opened up the door and there was Bruce, the guy who was in love with Rocky.

"Rocky isn't home. I'm not sure what time he's going to be back." I started shutting the door, but Bruce kicked the based with his foot to stop me from closing it.

"I'm not here for Rocky, Doc." He pushed the door open and came inside, closing it behind him.

"I know you saw us the other night. It was fucking hot. I got so turned on knowing you were watching your brother fuck me."

I played it off like I didn't know what he was talking about. He kept getting closer to me, and I could see his eyes going up and down my body, and I knew he knew I didn't have anything on under my shorts.

"Like I said, Rocky's not home. I'll let him know you..."

Bruce pushed me against the wall and started rubbing his hands up and down my chest. I looked down and could see my dick starting to sprout up in my shorts.

"I may be in love with your brother, but ever since the night you watched us fucking—I've been dreaming about which one of you could fuck me better."

He put his hands down my shorts and shoved his tongue down my throat. What if Rocky walked in and saw this? He honestly probably wouldn't even care. What if Jackie walked in? Did I even care at this point? Here I was with a hot guy playing with my balls and making out with me.

I pushed his face away from mine so I could talk. "The only way we're doing this is if you fuck me." I was still exhausted from the night before and really didn't feel like doing any of the work. Rocky got a smile on his face and came back in to make out with me again, and this time I could feel him grab the elastic of my shorts and push them down to the floor.

He grabbed onto my dick again and started stroking it, then dropped down to his knees to swallow me. He opened his wide mouth and pushed himself slowly down on my shaft until his lips met my body. I could feel the head of my cock pushing through the back of his throat. He didn't gag at all. He held his mouth there, and I could feel his tongue swirling around my cock. He came up for air, then started going back and forth, grabbing onto my balls and occasionally going down to suck on them. I held onto the back of his head and at one point took full control, shoving my dick as far into his mouth as I could.

At one point when he released my cock to take a breather, I turned around and arched my back, giving him easy access to my hole. I grabbed his head and pulled his face into my ass. I wanted to feel his tongue go as deep as my cock did in his mouth. He took his hands and spread my ass cheeks as wide as he could and licked all around the edges of my hole. I could tell he was teasing me to get me all worked up, and it was certainly working. I let him go in circles for a minute or two, then walked over to the couch and laid down on my back.

He ripped off his clothes as he followed me and got down on his stomach in front of me, diving right back into my hole. I grabbed onto his hair and made sure I kept him down there— he definitely knew what he was doing. I started rubbing his cock with my foot and could tell he was ready to go. I pulled him up toward me. "I want you inside of me now."

He spit on his hand and started rubbing it over the head of his penis. I picked up my legs and held them back, and he grabbed one of them and threw it over his shoulders. He held onto his dick and guided it toward my hole, gently pressing the head against it. He had me dripping wet from eating it, and his cock slid right inside, and damn did it feel amazing.

He slowly started rocking back and forth, letting me enjoy every inch that he had to offer. I could tell he knew what he was doing—pushing his cock in as far as he could and then pulling it out so slowly until the head was nearly peeking out, then pushing it back in. He did this for a minute or two, then just started going to town. I couldn't believe how incredible he felt as he shoved his monster in and out of my hole. I started jerking my own dick at the same rhythm he was fucking me, pulling his head down to mine so I could kiss him.

He must have fucked me for a good ten minutes, occasionally grabbing onto my cock and stroking it for me. I was getting close to blowing but wanted him to finish first, and as soon as I said I wanted him to fill my hole, I could feel his load releasing inside of me. His dick was throbbing so hard as he filled me up, and I pulled his torso closer to me to get all of it.

I told him to keep fucking me while I started jerking off, but he pulled his dick out, and I actually got mad for a second because I thought he was going to leave me hanging. He bent down in front of me and spit on my dick and started sucking on it, and I knew this was going to make me blow. I assumed he was just going to swallow me, but then he got up, straddled me, and lowered his ass down on my tool, slamming it into his hole. He started riding it so hard and so fast that I was exploding inside of him within five seconds. I let out quite the scream, and he leaned forward and started kissing me while I was still thrusting and unloading inside of him.

He lifted his body off mine, leaning forward and still kissing me, and I could feel my load dripping out of his hole onto my cock. He got down on the floor next to the couch and started sucking on my dick again, scooping up my load and swallowing it like a vacuum. I don't care what anyone says—when a guy does that, he's a keeper.

We made out for a few more minutes, and then I realized that we were still naked in the living room and that anyone could walk in at any moment. We both scrambled for our clothes, and I ran upstairs to get a shirt. As I came down the stairs, Bruce was heading toward the door, and just as he grabbed the door handle, it came flying open.

"Hey guys, what are you up to tonight?"

Rocky. So nonchalant, with no clue about what had just happened.

Chapter 5

With how busy I had been over the past few months, I was starting to think about just unplugging for a while and taking a vacation. It had been years since I had been to Europe, and I really wanted to get back, as every time I ever traveled there, I was always in a relationship. I could only imagine the situations I could get tangled in while traveling around as a single man. Plus, there was this place in Prague that I had seen in pornos before, and I really wanted to find out if it was real or just staged.

It was basically a sex house. You paid to get in, and as soon as you walked around the corner, there were holes everywhere. Guys lay with the top halves of their bodies hidden and their asses sticking out in any position you could imagine. And glory holes—everywhere. It didn't matter whether you wanted to get your dick sucked or actually wanted to bottom. And the great thing was—you could move around all you want. So, if I wanted to fuck some guy doggy style for a few minutes, and then move over to a glory hole to finish off with a blowjob, I could. That's at least how it works in the porn I've seen.

As much as I wanted to sit around and daydream about all of the sex adventures I could have in Europe as a single man, the weekend went by way too quickly. Monday came before I knew it, and I had a new patient coming into the office, so I needed to get in to do some extra preparation. The weekends always seemed to go by way too quickly, and I was starting to get to a point where I needed a break from my traditional sessions. I could only hope that my new patient had little knowledge about the type of therapy I use.

I checked my schedule and was surprised to see that I only had one patient coming in today, which was a bit odd for a Monday. I got everything prepared, and he arrived about 15 minutes after I got into the office. He looked awfully familiar, but I couldn't quite figure out where I knew him from. He introduced himself as Tony, and I led him back to the therapy room so we could begin our session.

"Tony, I'm glad you came in today. Why don't you tell me why you're here?"

Well, Doc. There's this guy that I've known for a few years now. We work at the same place and see each other at least four nights a week. We have a great friendship, but over the last few months, I've started developing feelings for him. I, actually, I think I might be in love with him, and we haven't even gone out on a date.

"Interesting. Tell me about this guy who has stolen your heart."

His name is Nicholas, and like I said, we've been working together for like three years. He is the most beautiful man I've ever seen. He's handsome and muscular. Holy shit is he muscular. His arms could crack a walnut, and I'd like to wash my clothes on his abs. He has an amazing ass, and his dick isn't too bad either.

He could tell I was thrown off about his dick comment and went on to explain.

Like, I've seen his penis, but never in a sexual way. We work at a strip club. We're both strippers, and we occasionally dance on stage together. When we're in the back, most guys just walk around naked, and his cock just swings around like a baby's arm. There've been so many times I've just wanted to drop onto my knees and devour that thing, which a lot of guys who work there do, but I'm always nervous about how he might react.

"Have you ever talked to him about any of this or discussed maybe going on a date?"

I'm always too nervous to bring it up to him. We work at a strip club. Most guys who are in this line of work don't get into relationships. It's just way too messy. And at our strip club, there are sex rooms, and we're expected to do "extra" for our VIP guests. I'm into having the occasional threesome or orgy, but I don't want an open relationship, and I'm not sure I could be in one with someone who I know is going into the next room to give some old rich guy a BJ. I just really need help figuring all of this out. I want to be with him, and if that means I have to quit my job, then I would, but I'm not sure that he would want to do the same thing. He's not the brightest guy, so he really needs to use his assets to make a living. I'm just so stuck.

"Well, Tony. I think what we need to do is maybe try to get him here for a session with you. This is a safe space where you can speak freely, and I'm sure if he is who you say he is, he will be open to your thoughts. Let's set up a session for both of you for this Friday. But in the meantime, I want you to do this. Do you guys work together again before this Friday?

Yes, we are working together tonight, and we are actually doing the final act together.

"Okay, before you go on stage, when he's walking around the back room, I need you to drop down and give him that BJ like you've always wanted to. But don't let him cum. Get him close enough that you know he's about to blow, and then just stop. Then, go do your dance, and when you're finished, see how he reacts and what happens next. I guarantee between the edging of the blowjob and the dance, he won't be able to resist you. And then, when you come on Friday, we can discuss and go from there."

Tony thanked me and went running out the door. I imagine he would be heading straight to work to get started on his assignment. I started filing his paperwork and realized I didn't even ask which club he worked at—part of me wanted to go tonight to see what his dynamic was on stage with this Nick guy.

Chapter 6

As I was locking up the office, my phone started going off, but my hands were full, and I just ignored it. But whoever was on the other side didn't care because they just kept blowing it up and obviously wanted to get my attention and quickly.

"Come spend the night. My wife is out of town."

It was Mike, the married guy who came over and fucked me a few weeks earlier. I figured I would have been hearing from him at some point but didn't think he would actually follow through with his invite. So, I thought, *What the hell?* When was I ever going to get this chance again? He sent me his address, and I headed over to his place.

Mike lived in a gorgeous house up in the hills overlooking the bay. I was a little surprised because I had no clue he owned a home like this and actually had no idea what he did for work. I walked up to the door and rang the doorbell, and as soon as he answered, he gave me a huge hug and a kiss on the lips.

"I'm so excited. I mean, glad you could make it. My wife never goes out of town, so as soon as she left, I knew I needed to call you!"

He gave me a tour of his house, which had to have been at least 5,000 square feet. We ended back in the kitchen, and I sat down at the island. He poured us each a glass of wine, and he sat down next to me and started rubbing my leg. We made small talk for a while, and he was really flirtatious. This was a bit of a different side of him from how he acted when he came over in the middle of the night to fuck. I started to realize that he was obviously gay but had to hide it and stay married as his cover story.

He gulped down his glass of wine and grabbed the back of my head, pulling me forward to kiss me. As I leaned in, I knocked my wine glass over, and he didn't even seem to notice. We started making out in the kitchen, him holding tightly onto the back of my head and me hanging onto the front of his shirt. We probably made out for ten minutes when he stopped and grabbed onto my hand, leading me up the stairs to his bedroom.

His room had floor to ceiling windows overlooking the bay, and the lights reflecting on the water created a bit of a romantic feeling. He flipped a switch on the wall, and the fireplace at the end of the bed turned on. He told me to make myself comfortable, and that he was going to take a quick shower.

When I heard the shower turn on, I hopped in the middle of the bed with my arms behind my head, and I damn near sank into its softness. His bed felt like I was floating in a cloud. I'm assuming he wanted to really clean out, because I had every intention on trying to fuck his hole tonight, and after a few minutes I decided to sneak into the shower with him.

I walked into the bathroom and could see that he had his back to me, so I took off my clothes and slowly slipped inside the shower. I got up behind him and wrapped my arms around him, pulling his body into mine. He reached around and grabbed onto the back of my head again, and I started kissing his neck, feeling his ass move from side to side, rubbing on my cock. He bent forward and arched his back, basically invite me to get inside of him, but I didn't want that yet. I dropped down and spread his cheeks and started eating his ass, shoving my tongue as far in as I could. He started moaning and told me he had never had his ass eaten before, and as soon as I heard that,

I shoved my finger in and started licking fast and hard. I wanted him to enjoy every second.

I stood up and flipped him around, pushing his shoulders down until he was on his knees in front of me. I was holding onto the base on my cock, and I grabbed the back of his head and pulled his face to me. He opened up his mouth and willingly accepted my monster, bobbing his head back and forth on it. This was the guy who damn near made me blow from a blowjob before, and he was on his way to doing it again. As soon as I felt that I was going to cum, I pulled him up toward me and held him tight, making out with him again. I shut off the shower water, and we dried off and headed back to the bed.

I laid down and he got on top of me, letting the weight of his ripped body press against mine. He was holding me on my sides, kissing me, while I pressed my fingers into his ass cheeks. I wanted to be inside of him so badly, and I knew he wanted the same.

He leaned over and grabbed the lube off his nightstand and poured a generous amount on my cock, stroking it to cover the entire thing. He threw one of his legs over me and slowly lowered himself onto my throbbing dick. I held onto the base of it until he grabbed it to guide it in. I felt the head press against his pulsating hole, and he lowered himself onto me, inch by inch. I could see from the look on his face that he was in pain. He stopped about mid-shaft and just looked at me with a smile. "This is the first time I've ever bottomed."

I figured he had never bottomed, although obviously being secretly gay, it wasn't a given. He lowered himself the rest of the way and told me not to move for a moment so he could get used to me being inside of him. I reached over and grabbed the poppers off the table, sniffing them before handing over to him. He took a huge breath of the scent, then threw the bottle and slowly started moving himself back and forth on top of me. I wanted to be gentle, although I also wanted to just start drilling him. His hole around my pole was like a vacuum— he was fucking tight.

He placed his hands on my chest to prop himself up, and I held onto his hips while he rocked back and forth. I wanted to give him full control until I felt him lean forward, and I knew that was my invitation. I began thrusting my cock in and out of his hole, and the screams coming from his mouth told me that he was loving every pump. I could feel myself getting close to blowing, and I grabbed onto Mike and rolled over to get him on his back. I grabbed his legs, held them in the air, and started pounding away at his hole while he began jerking off. I could feel myself about to blow, and I let out a huge scream as that first shot of cum shot deep inside of him. As soon as he felt my jizz, he started blowing his load all over, shooting straight over his head.

I leaned forward and started kissing him again, making my way down his chest and to his cock, licking up all of his cum I could find. I rolled over onto the side of him and reached my arms around him, holding him as closely and as tightly as I could.

We fell asleep, and I can't even count how many times throughout the night that I woke up to him sucking my cock, or he woke up to me fingering his hole and jerking him off, and I'm guessing we probably fucked four more times before the sun came up.

And yes, we took turns plowing each other's holes.

Chapter 7

I went from Mike's house straight into the office the following day, and I couldn't stop thinking about my night with him. This was always the one downside to sleeping with married men—you don't have a chance with them. But that was also the one positive thing too—you don't have a chance with them. So, it's typically a quick, easy fuck, and married men are typically great in bed because they get to live out all their pent-up fantasies with you, and then you can move on and not worry about catching feelings. Although sometimes you do.

I got to the office, checked my schedule, and saw that I had another new client coming in—Pete. There was no additional information with the appointment notes, so all I could do was wait to see who showed up. I continued working on notes from my appointment with Tony, and then I heard the front door open.

I assumed this was Pete. And he looked awfully familiar, but I couldn't quite pinpoint it. I introduced myself, and we made a bit of small talk before moving into the therapy room. When he sat down, he looked at me and smiled and mentioned that he saw me at the mall last week. And that's when I remembered who he was. He was the "can't wait to see you next week" cute guy who ran up to me at the mall.

I set my notebook down because I somehow already knew where this was going.

"So, what brings you in here? What can I help you with?"

Honestly, I know you're a sex therapist, and that's what I need help with. I'm having a lot of trouble figuring out if I'm a top or a bottom. Like, I'm not sure how you actually figure it out.

I wasn't sure if this guy was pulling my leg, or if he was actually having issues with this. Like, he was super cute, hot actually, and obviously wouldn't have any issues getting probably any guy he wanted. Was he here to get help, or was he making this shit up to just get in my pants?

"Tell me a little bit about your sex life. It can be difficult to figure out what we like and what we want to do. Tell me about your experiences."

Well, nobody knows I'm gay. I've only dated girls, but I've never actually had sex with one. I'm still a virgin. I know I'm gay—I'm super attracted to you, I mean guys.

He blushed when he slipped and said me. I can't lie. I smiled a little bit.

I want to figure out what my position is. There's so much pressure to be one way or another, and I need help figuring it out.

"You know, there's no rule book on how this sort of thing goes. You don't have to be one way or the other. You can be both. You can be neither. It's entirely up to you."

I really want to figure this out. I'm ready to come out to my family. I'm ready to start dating guys, figure out what I like, meet someone, and fall in love. I'm ready to have sex.

There it was. This guy obviously just wanted to fuck, and he knew with my treatments that this would get him exactly what he wanted. I got up out of my seat, moved over to the couch, and sat down next to him.

"I'm here to help you through this. What do you want?"

He looked down at the zipper on my pants and moved his hand onto my leg. He didn't have to answer my question because I already knew what he wanted. I unzipped my pants, reached in, and pulled my soft cock out. I held onto the base of it and waited for him to make the next move.

"Is this what you want?"

He looked at me with a grin and dropped down onto his knees in front of the couch, leaning down to lick the head of my penis. I sat back and threw my hands up behind the couch. He moved his mouth down my shaft, then grabbed on and started stroking it while he sucked. He lost attention pretty quickly because after about thirty seconds, he stood up and pulled his pants down, exposing his massive ten inches in front of my face.

I leaned forward and started jerking him off, sucking on his balls before moving my tongue up his shaft to the head and back down to the base. I wrapped my lips around that monster and started choking on it, enjoying every push against the back of my throat that he could offer me. Man, I really did enjoy sucking cock.

I got up after a few minutes and pushed him into the couch, his knees bent on the edge and his head hanging over the back of it.

I leaned in and started eating his hole, and he let out moans of pure enjoyment. I wanted to get him nice and wet so I could get inside of him, and I reached around a few times to make sure he was still hard.

"You want it raw?" He turned around and nodded his head. I lubed up his hole and my cock, and went to slowly insert it into his hole, but his hole was actually pretty loose, and it kind of just sucked me in.

Just as I thought. He wasn't a virgin. He was looser than a bolt about to fall off.

I didn't care though. He was hot and wanted some action, and I was still worked up from my adventures just a few hours before. I had planned on taking it pretty gently with him, but now that I could tell he was a pro, I went to town on his hole, pounding his ass as hard as I could and thrusting my dick deep inside of him. He was backing himself into me, almost as if I couldn't fuck him hard enough. He let me go at his hole for about five or six minutes before turning around and asking if he could fuck me.

Normally I would have said yes, but his warm hole was just what I needed, and I didn't want to lose any momentum. "You can schedule another session for that." I pushed his head down into the couch and started pounding as hard as I could.

I could tell he was stroking his cock pretty quickly, and I heard him let out a loud moan as he shot his load all over the couch. I asked him if he wanted my load, and he nodded his head, so I grabbed onto his hips and gave a few more thrusts inside of him until I released everything I had in his hole. It honestly couldn't have been much, as I was certainly drained from my night with Mike, but it definitely felt like quite a bit, and I saw a little drip out as I pulled out of him.

I probably should have let him fuck me with his monster cock, but sure enough, he scheduled another appointment before he left, and I knew this would be one patient I'd be more than happy to see again.

Chapter 8

After that session, I really didn't feel like seeing any other patients, so I cleared my schedule and headed home. I had every intention of just relaxing and going to bed early, but as I was scrolling through Instagram, I saw another ad for Swinging Richards for their nightly event. One of the guys in the post was obviously Nick, but I couldn't tell who the other guy was, because all I could see was his ass—but it sure was a sweet one.

I decided to go, just for a little bit, secretly hoping I could get some alone time with Nick or that maybe he'd want to come over. Maybe it was a sign that this ad popped up on my feed, or maybe I'd end up in another orgy like last time.

I got to the club and grabbed my usual drink from my usual spot, waiting for the show to start. A bunch of different guys were on stage doing their little dances, but none of them even came close to turning me on the way that Nick did. I was also super curious who the other guy in the ad was, and more importantly, who that fine ass belonged to. I assumed it was someone who would be dancing with Nick tonight.

Nick came out on stage with nothing on but his cock in a sock, and a few minutes later, the other guy came out and up behind him, pushing Nick forward and grinding on his ass. I had to move to a different spot at the bar because the light was shining in my eyes, and I dropped my drink on the floor when I realized who it was that Nick was dancing with.

It was Tony. My patient. And the Nicholas that he was referring to was Nick. My Nick.

I couldn't believe what I was seeing. I'm not sure how I didn't put two and two together and figure out when he was talking about a stipper named Nicholas, and describing the features of his body, that it was my Nick. I started walking toward the door, but then decided to stay and see what kind of chemistry they had together.

Honestly, I wish that I had left because it was clear that the two of them made magic together. Watching them intertwining themselves together on stage—grinding each other, feeling each other, kissing each other—it was actually kind of magical. I looked around, and they really knew how to get the crowd going. I noticed a few guys rubbing their dicks, several people running off to the orgy rooms, and even saw a guy in the corner watching the stage while he was getting his dick sucked. I even felt myself getting a boner, which I wanted to take care of, but I didn't want to miss out on what was happening off stage.

The show ended, and Nick and Tony disappeared into the background. I went back to my spot at the bar, and I heard someone yell my name.

"Dr. Cage. I can't believe you came! I want you to meet someone!"

It was Tony, and that someone he wanted me to meet was Nick. He grabbed Nick and pulled him up to me to introduce us, and I pretended like I didn't know who he was.

"Nicholas, this is my therapist that I was telling you about! Doc, I can't believe you came."

I shook Nick's hand and just played it cool, although anyone could have seen the tension between us. Nick was somehow reading my mind because he was also trying to keep cool.

I turned around back to the bar and ordered another drink. I noticed the manager come running from the stage and whisper into Tony's ear.

"Fuck. I'm sorry, guys. One of my VIPs just came in. Nicholas, I'll see you later. Doc, can't wait for my next session!" Tony ran down the hallway and greeted some old man, and the two disappeared into one of the rooms.

Nick and I just looked at each other and laughed, then he leaned in to give me a hug.

"I'm not sure what that was abou...."

I interrupted him before he could even finish. "I'm paying for a VIP room. How do I get a VIP room?"

Nick looked confused and tried talking me out of it.

"No, I want you. Now."

Nick walked away and grabbed the credit card terminal. I handed him my card and didn't even care how much it was going to cost. I needed him this minute and couldn't wait a moment longer. I signed the receipt, and he grabbed me by the hand and led me into his room.

The minute he slammed the door shut, I threw him against the wall and started making out with him. We were ripping each other's clothes off until we were completely naked, as if we had never seen each other before. His body was like a temple, chiseled, rock hard, and his cock was perfect. I remembered sucking it once before, and this time I was going to get the entire thing.

He dropped down with his back against the wall and started sucking on my dick. I grabbed the back of his head, thrusting myself into his face, causing him to grab onto my cock to be able to breathe a little bit. I knew this moment was only going to last for a few minutes, but I wanted it to last for hours.

I let him suck on my tool for a few minutes before trading spots with him. I pulled him up and gave him a quick kiss and then dropped down to devour his piece. I could barely get the entire thing in my mouth but was determined to feel him choke me. I felt him pressing against the back of my throat and loved every second of it. I could have sat there and sucked on his perfect cock for hours—it's dicks like his that make people want to be gay in the first place. No wonder he did so well at the club.

He pulled me up off the ground, and I could tell he wanted my ass. He started kissing me again as we made our way over to the couch. I could only imagine the stains that were on this couch–luckily it was damn near pitch black in the VIP rooms.

He pushed me down on the couch on my stomach and drove his face right into my ass, licking up and down against my hole and spreading my cheeks to get in as deep as he could. I stopped him for a minute so I could turn over and get on my back, and he propped my legs on his shoulders and dove right back down. I started stroking my cock and he was licking my hole, and he shoved a few fingers inside to really get it nice and open for him.

He came up for some air and I pulled his face to mine, making out with him again. I kept my knees propped up toward my shoulders, and as he leaned forward to kiss me, I grabbed ahold of his cock and guided him inside of me. He never lost focus of kissing me while I steered his dick toward my landing strip, and before I knew it, he was completely inside of me, still focusing on his lips against mine.

"Fuck me."

He grabbed onto my legs and started moving his hips forward and backward, getting a little faster, a little deeper, a little harder with each move. I could feel him spreading my hole out with his massive dick, and it put me in a feeling of pure ecstasy. I kind of felt the way I did the night before with Mike, like there was nowhere else I'd rather be.

He fucked me like this for a few minutes, and then I pushed him onto his back on the other end of the couch so I could ride him. I got on top of him and sat right down on his dick and started bouncing up and down, him holding onto my hips and helping with each bounce. He started stroking my cock while still inside of me and told me to shoot my load as far as I could. He opened his mouth and stuck out his tongue, and I started blowing my load all over his chest and up into his mouth. I leaned down and licked some of it up with my tongue, holding it and moving over to start making out with him.

He grabbed my hips and raised my ass a little bit to get a better angle so he could start pounding at my hole, and within seconds, I could feel him filling me up. He lowered himself back down and I kept bouncing up and down, draining his vein of everything he had. I leaned forward, started kissing him again, and whispered in his ear that I wanted to see him again.

We cleaned each other off, and I opened the door and peeked out to make sure Tony wasn't around. I walked out of the room and toward the bar, and just as I turned the corner I turned around and saw Tony come out of his VIP room.

"Damn, I didn't think you'd still be here, Doc. You know, we have some pretty sweet rooms back here. I'm sure one of the dancers would love to have you!"

I certainly was flattered, and based on the conversation, it was evident that he had no clue what had just happened. I looked over his shoulder and saw Nick sneak out of the room, winking to me as he ran the other direction.

"Thanks, Tony, but I already got what I needed tonight."

Author Bio

Grayson Ace has had his fair share of sexcapades, and figured why not write about them? Recently divorced, he is re-discovering himself (and plenty of hot men) and creating many new sexy adventures along the way. If you like what you see, please leave a review, and you never know....you may end up in one of the stories!

GraysonAce.com
Facebook: Grayson Ace
Instagram: graysonaceofficial
Twitter: @GraysonAce1

More Books From

Grayson Ace

How I Got Here
First Year Out of the Closet
You're Only a Top?
You're Only a Bottom?
I Think I'm a Serial Swiper
Lookin' in All the Wrong Places
What Makes Me a Whore?
A Breach in Confidentiality
Back Door Pass
My European Adventure
An Unexpected Affair
More to come!

4 Horsemen Publications

LGBT Erotica

Leo Sparx

Before Alexander
Claiming Alexander
Taming Alexander
Saving Alexander

Erotica

Ali Whippe

Office Hours
Tutoring Center
Athletics
Extra Credit
Bound for Release
Fetish Circuit

Dalia Lance

My Home on Whore Island
Slumming It on Slut Street
Training of the Tramp
The Imperfect Perfection
72% Match
It Was Meant To Be... Or Whatever

Chastity Veldt

Molly in Milwaukee
Irene in Indianapolis
Lydia in Louisville
Natasha in Nashville
Alyssa in Atlanta

Honey Cummings

Sleeping with Sasquatch
Cuddling with Chupacabra
Naked with New Jersey Devil
Laying with the Lady in Blue
Wanton Woman in White
Beating it with Bloody Mary
Beau and Professor Bestialora
The Goat's Gruff
Goldie and Her Three Beards
Pied Piper's Pipe
Princess Pea's Bed
Jack's Beanstalk

4HorsemenPublications.com

www.ingramcontent.com/pod-product-compliance
Lightning Source LLC
Chambersburg PA
CBHW050501110726
47899CB00003B/1027